D1090704
בס״ד
לד׳ הארץ ומלואה
From the Library of:
Please read it to me!

by Risa Rotman
illustrated by Tova Leff

Dedicated by Michael and Ellen Goldberg
In honor of their daughter Arlyn's bat mitzvah
And in honor of their other children, Jesse and Jonah.

Fit for a Princess

In loving memory of my mother, Henna Hitza bas Eliyahu (Mrs. Anne Dodick) a'h... a woman who refused to be bound by the dictates of the fashion world. R.R.

To my *two little princesses, Esti and Nechama Leba. T.L.*

First Edition 2008 / 5768

Editor: D.L. Rosenfeld
Managing Editor: Yossi Leverton
Layout: Eli Chaikin

ISBN 13: 978-1-929628-38-4
ISBN 10: 1-929628-38-2
LCCN: 2007932113

HACHAI PUBLISHING
Brooklyn, New York
Tel: 718-633-0100 Fax: 718-633-0103
www.hachai.com info@hachai.com

Printed in Hong Kong

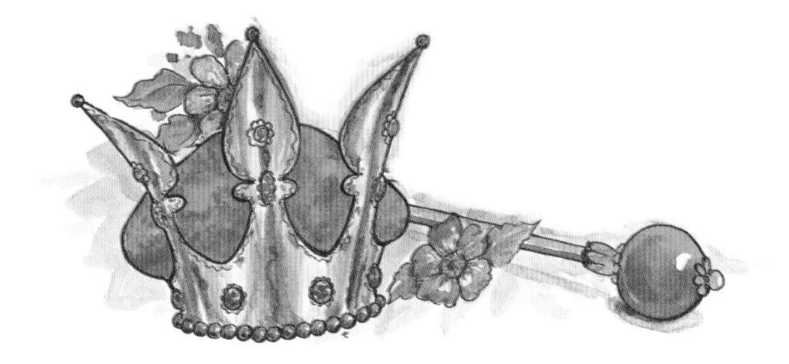

Once upon a time, there was a princess who lived in a royal palace. Like most princesses, she wore a long, swishy gown and a bright, shiny crown.

But, unlike most
princesses, she didn't
spend her time looking in the
mirror, or counting her money, or
playing with golden toys.

She was known as "The Busy Princess,"
because her father, the King, gave her
some very important jobs to do.

The princess was in charge of the royal library.

She made sure that little children had plenty of colorful picture books, and that students had whatever they needed for their studies. She took good care of the royal books, and put them away in their proper places.

This wasn't an easy job, because sometimes, her swishy gown would get caught on the corner of a shelf, and someone would have to help untangle it. Sometimes, when the princess reached up high to get a special book for someone, her golden crown would slide off and go rolling across the room.

The princess's other important job was tending the royal gardens. She made sure the gardeners planted only the healthiest flowers and trees.

She helped them
water the plants,
pull out the
weeds, and trim
the bushes.

That wasn't an easy job either, because sometimes her golden crown would slip down over her eyes while she was watering. Often, the princess would trip on the hem of her swishy gown and fall right onto the wet grass!

Finally the princess decided that she couldn't work in her gown and her crown. She'd have to save them for special occasions.

But what then should a princess wear?
Quickly, she called her royal advisors and asked for some advice.

The first advisor to step forward
was an advisor from the west.
"Dear Princess," she said, "I know what
would be just right for you. Why not
wear a flowery dress with a ruffle
and a long white apron?

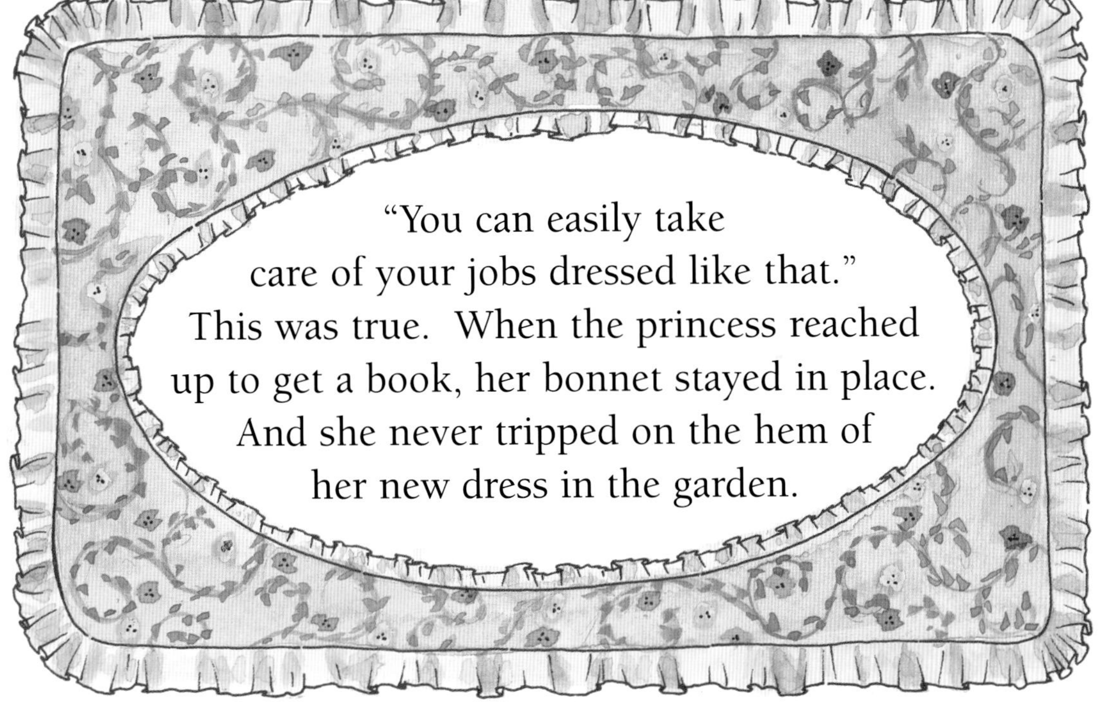

"You can easily take
care of your jobs dressed like that."
This was true. When the princess reached
up to get a book, her bonnet stayed in place.
And she never tripped on the hem of
her new dress in the garden.

But the people of the kingdom forgot to curtsey and say, “Good morning, your Royal Highness,” with the princess dressed like that.

She simply didn’t look much like a princess anymore.

The Busy Princess gathered her advisors once again. This time an advisor from the east stepped forward. “Honorable Princess, I know what would be just right for you.

“Why not wear a long straight robe, an umbrella-shaped hat, and tiny silk shoes? Then you will look delicate and gracious.”

That was true.
When the princess went out,
she looked like a lovely
visitor from the east.

But no one in the kingdom
recognized her, so they still didn't
call her, "Your Royal Highness,"
or curtsey at all.

Each day,
the advisors came
to the princess with
more ideas.

“Skirts and shirts with silver buttons from the north!”
“Flowery dresses with straw hats from the south!”

It all became very confusing.

The princess realized that the advisors wanted her to wear their own favorite kinds of clothes, their own favorite colors, their own favorite styles.

The princess looked in
the mirror and said,
"What would my father
be proud to see me wear?
I need clothing that
is graceful and
dignified, beautiful
and neat."

"Wherever I go,
I want to look like the
daughter of a king."

Without wasting a moment, the Busy Princess took a careful look through her royal closet.

She pulled out this and put on that, until – at last, her outfit was complete.

From then on, everyone could see exactly what was fit for a princess.

Dear Jewish Daughter,
We can be proud to
dress in our own unique
way, because we are
all daughters of
Hashem, our King.